Jethro's
Journey Back to
Grandmommy's
Ocean

Jethro's
Journey Back to
Grandmommy's
Ocean

Susan Shaw Rhyne

Illustrated by
Cornelia Knight and Eva Crawford

XULON PRESS

Xulon Press
2301 Lucien Way #415
Maitland, FL 32751
407.339.4217
www.xulonpress.com

© 2020 by Susan Shaw Rhyne
Illustrated by Cornelia Knight and Eva Crawford

Printed in the United States of America.

ISBN-13: 978-1-6312-9096-1

Dedication

To my mother, Edith Galloway Shaw, the best grandmommy ever. She was mother to eight children and grandmother to nineteen grandchildren. She showed her love of family through her hospitality and excellent cooking. I am so thankful she taught me how to cook and for her treasured recipes. A lover of seashells and pelicans, she welcomed us all to Grandmommy's Ocean in Jacksonville Beach, Florida.

The sun was just beginning to lighten the cove at the lake where I had been resting for several weeks. The animals began to awaken and make their welcoming sounds. The birds were chirping their "good mornings" to each other. Bees were buzzing around the flowers on the decks, and Norma and her young mallard ducklings were quietly swimming around the cove, looking for breakfast. The babies made soft quacking sounds to let their mother know they were following her. I had grown quite fond of waking up to these sounds over the last few weeks. It had not always been this way.

Thinking of earlier times, I remembered days of landing on the warm waves of the ocean, hoping to spot a school of minnows to eat. In fact, I remember the day I received my name. That was the day I saw a kind-looking lady walking on the beach, with her small bucket and hand-held net, looking for seashells.

The young children near her called her Grandmommy. She noticed me circle above her. When she caught several minnows in her net, she threw some of them to me. I followed behind her on the beach for a while. She turned to walk back to her family when she spotted me again. We quietly watched each other, but then she said, "Thank you for walking with me today. I think I will call you Jethro." That was a sweet memory. I am now so homesick for the ocean and beaches of home.

Being a young, brown pelican, I was a long way from my home. I was used to warm, sandy beaches near the ocean. My brothers and I had learned to fly near our mother's nest in that humid wetland in the south. Things had gone tragically wrong when the big, windy storm blew across our grasslands, when the hot days were getting shorter.

As we were trying to get to safety, I was caught up in the whirlwinds and blown way off course. I did not recognize where I landed...or rather was dumped...in the woody area away from home. I guessed I was lucky to be alive when I saw all of the trees stripped of their leaves, some broken off several feet from the ground. Trees were thrown on houses. Power lines were lying across roads, houses, and cars.

My abrupt landing injured my wing and left foot. I was so grateful that I was found by one of the rangers at the Raptor Center.

Ranger Robby took me to this refuge and helped feed me and bind up my foot and wing. He was kind to me and even found young minnows for me to eat. There were other birds there, but none of them looked like me. I wondered if I would ever see my family again. Where were they, and which way should I go to find them?

After a time of healing, I realized that Ranger Robby and his friends were letting some of the injured birds go into the wild. When would it be my turn? My foot felt pretty good, but my wing was still bound. I could not fly. I would try to eat more and get stronger.

Finally, my day came. Ranger Robby took me to the nearby lake and let me go. I was pretty wobbly at first, but soon I gained my balance. I could only fly for a short period of time, since I got tired. That was when I found the cove on the big lake where Norma and her ducklings lived. I rested there for several weeks and realized that I enjoyed being around other water animals for a change.

Finding my perch on a post in the cove, I could rest there and feel safe. I also found out there was a good bit of activity going on, and that amused me. There was a dock with several places for boats on the side.

The man, who I heard called Captain Roy, would walk down to the dock in the mornings to check on things while he drank his coffee. He wouldn't stay long and left soon after going back to the house. He and his mate had three girls that loved being on the water.

The sisters, all young girls, would come down to the water later in the day. Captain Roy had bought them a little Sunfish to sail in the cove. They had such a good time sailing around together. The little sailboat was not designed to take all three of them on the water at the same time.

However, they would all try to get in the sailboat and, most times, they would flip it over. You have never heard such laughing, squealing, and giggling! Their joy reminded me of the fun my brothers and I had flying and fishing together.

A few days later, I had just about talked myself into trying to find my way back to Grandmommy's Ocean, when a family showed up on the dock. The mother was there with her three children. She brought her lounge chair, towels, and a book. The older boys were very active and comfortable in the water, playing on the inner tubes and floats, but the young girl was not a good swimmer.

Although she was wearing a life vest, the mother still did not feel comfortable letting her jump into the deep water like she wanted to do.

Seeing a rope on the dock, the mother tied it to the back buckle on the life vest and tied the other end to her chair. This safety feature allowed the child to jump in the water to her heart's delight.". The mother could get to her quickly, if needed, but it granted the young girl the freedom to jump into the water and play around, as her brothers were doing.

They also played with the big, brown dog named Max. The boys would throw a ball, and he would jump off the side of the dock to retrieve it. Then he would climb up the rock border to get back to the dock. When the boys got tired of throwing the ball, he would drop it on the chair for the mother to throw. She would toss it backwards over her head and off Max would go. He would never give up. Even when she hid the ball from him, he would bring a stick for her to throw. Some of his sticks were like logs of lumber. Max was determined to play the entire time they were there. They all had a wonderful time on the lake.

Several days later, I finally said goodbye to Norma and her ducklings, and headed south in the direction of home. I was not sure how far I needed to go. I flew over fields and trees until I would come to small lakes or ponds. I knew I had to keep looking for a large body of water, so I kept going.

After going through a town with two big bridges, I flew a ways farther out to the big body of water that I thought I wanted. I needed to rest, so I landed on the jetty rocks where houses were right on the beach. While watching the three closest houses, a female pelican flew up near me. She had been watching the families playing on the beach and going up the stairs to the deck, where young people were throwing balls filled with water. It seemed to be a contest between the boys and the girls. Once again, there was a great deal of laughing and squealing when the balls popped. My friend and I watched until the young people went inside all three houses. What a big family!!

I turned to the young pelican beside me and asked her what her name was. She said, "I don't have a name." I told her, "My name is Jethro. I think you need a name. I will call you Penelope." She seemed to like that name. We started looking for fish for our dinner.

Some of the guys came out to the jetties to fish for a while. They offered some of the small fish to Penelope and me. We were grateful.

The next day, we saw all of the cars out front being packed up. We decided it was time to move on as well. Penelope agreed to travel with me, since she thought she knew the way. I was grateful for the company.

The next morning, we started out looking for the thin waterway where small ships could travel in calm waters. After several days of flying, we found the thin ribbon of water that we could follow. I was starting to get discouraged, but Penelope assured me that we were on the right track. Penelope sure knew her waterways.

As we reached the large bridge over the waterway, I realized that I recognized the area. I could see the ocean from the bridge. I raced ahead of Penelope to the fishing pier that was located at Grandmommy's Ocean.

Many people were on the beach that afternoon. Resting from our trip, we watched the families play on the beach. Children were playing with sand buckets and shovels, balls, and frisbees, and riding the waves with their rubber floats. One family had their red dog on the beach with them. They would throw a tennis ball to him, and he would retrieve it. Sometimes they would throw it out in the water and he would swim to get it, but he would head in the wrong direction from shore. The older girls would then put him up on their rafts to rest a while and, eventually, let him ride in to shore with the waves. They did that over and over again.

As some people were leaving the beach for the day, I noticed an older couple walking down to the big family. It was Grandmommy and Granddaddy. She was coming to look for seashells along the edge of the water, and he was bringing his big net to catch fish. This was my kind of fun. He enlisted the help of the young people to hold the big net and wade out in the water as far as they could go. The tallest ones had to go out in the deepest waters. As they hauled the net in to shore, Penelope and I could see what they brought in. The smallest fish were thrown back into the water, but I was good at finding those fish quickly. Penelope and I ate well that afternoon.

The smaller children and some visitors watched as this routine was followed over and over. One little girl played with the bucket in which the net had been brought. Her mom filled the bucket with sea water, and she dipped it out with a sand bucket. She even sat in the bucket to entertain herself. One of the little boys with a sunburned face ran up to Grandmommy and told her, "Look, Grandmommy, it's Jethro." She turned and waved to me. We had visited many days on her beach, and I enjoyed her company.

As the sun was setting, the family started to gather their buckets and shovels, balls, and rafts. Towels and blankets were shaken, and chairs were rinsed in the water. Beach bags helped carry their things, and everyone helped Granddaddy get his net back in the bucket. Grandmommy was happy. She had gone in the water for a short time. Her girls held on to her. She was short and could easily be knocked down by the waves. They all had taken good care of her.

We could see that she was pleased. Her family had once again come to her ocean. She enjoyed seeing them with rosy cheeks and sunburned shoulders, arms, and legs. As they all trudged across the sand and up the walkway into the sunset, I realized that summer must be almost over. Grandmommy's family would be leaving soon.

As we watched the parade of families exit the beach, I saw shadows of some objects flying toward us. I turned and realized it was my two younger brothers. They recognized me. They had grown a little and their feathers were darker. They told me that our family's nest was nearby and insisted that there were plenty of minnows for all of us. They flew off to go tell the rest of my family that I was home.

Perhaps next year Penelope would still be here, and I would once again see everyone come back to Grandmommy's Ocean. I was looking forward to seeing all of my family. It was good to finally be home.

Acknowledgements

I want to thank some of the many people that helped make <u>Jethro's Journey Back to Grandmommy's Ocean</u> become a reality.

I want to express my sincere gratitude to Eva Compton Crawford and her thirteen-year-old art student, Cornelia Knight for the excellent artwork they did to enhance my book. Eva has been a family friend since she was a baby. It is exciting to see that she inherited her artistic talent from her father. Thank you, Cornelia and Eva, for your extraordinary work.

To my five sisters, I want to say thank you for the memories we created at Grandmommy's Ocean. My children, Jimmy,

Patrick, and Jennifer and their cousins were instrumental in creating this story. Thank you, Jennifer, for all of your proofreading help and IT service.

Thank you to my friends for their encouragement. It is a wonderful feeling knowing that I have a cheerleading team urging me onward. Thank you, peeps!

This book is for my grandchildren: Robby, Davis, Katie, Ruby, and Sterling. May you continue to love books, and always love to journey to Grandmommy's Ocean.

And to my husband who has been by my side throughout our own journey of fifty-one years. Thank you for your support, care during illness, and running the house when I choose to write. Thank you, Jim. We are a good team. My heart is yours.

CPSIA information can be obtained
at www.ICGtesting.com
Printed in the USA
LVHW070605220420
654263LV00019B/939